DRAGON STORM

CARA AND SILVERTHIEF

Alastair Chisholm

illustrated by Eric Deschamps

A STEPPING STONE BOOK™

Random House 🏠 New York

Also in the series:

TOM AND IRONSKIN

Coming soon:

ELLIS AND PATHSEEKER

MIRA AND FLAMETELLER

CONTENTS

Text copyright © 2022 by Alastair Chisholm
Cover art and interior illustrations copyright © 2022 by Eric Deschamps

All rights reserved. Published in the United States by Random House Children's Books, a division of Penguin Random House LLC, New York. Originally published in paperback in slightly different form in the United Kingdom by Nosy Crow, Ltd, London, in 2022.

Random House and the colophon are registered trademarks and A Stepping Stone Book and the colophon are trademarks of Penguin Random House LLC.

Visit us on the Web!
rhcbooks.com

Educators and librarians, for a variety of teaching tools, visit us at RHTeachersLibrarians.com

Library of Congress Cataloging-in-Publication Data is available upon request.
ISBN 978-0-593-47957-5 (trade) — ISBN 978-0-593-47958-2 (lib. bdg.) — ISBN 978-0-593-47959-9 (ebook)

Printed in the United States of America
10 9 8 7 6 5 4 3 2 1
First American Edition

Random House Children's Books supports the
First Amendment and celebrates the right to read.

Penguin Random House LLC supports copyright. Copyright fuels creativity, encourages diverse voices, promotes free speech, and creates a vibrant culture. Thank you for buying an authorized edition of this book and for complying with copyright laws by not reproducing, scanning, or distributing any part in any form without permission. You are supporting writers and allowing Penguin Random House to publish books for every reader.

IN THE LAND OF DRACONIS, THERE ARE NO DRAGONS.

Once, there were. Once, humans
and dragons were friends and guarded
the land. They were wise, and strong, and
created the great city of Rivven together.

But then came the Dragon Storm, and the
dragons retreated from the world
of humans. To the men and women of
Draconis, they became legend and myth.

And so, these days, in the land of Draconis,
there are no dragons. . . .

Or so people thought.

1
THE SILVER THIEF

In the dead dark of a moonless night, a young girl climbed the palace walls.

The palace stood on an ancient rock that rose high above the city of Rivven. Its walls were well made, crafted from smooth gray stone with a few handholds. The girl moved confidently, ignoring the drop below her. Finding a crack between two stones, she pulled herself up and placed her feet onto a thin ledge. She reached for the next gap.

Wait.

The voice came from inside her head. She didn't know how or whose voice it was, but she'd heard it her whole life. It was her only friend, and she trusted it. She stopped. Above her, a guard leaned out over the edge of the wall and gazed down, bored. The girl waited, hidden in a gray cloak that perfectly matched the stonework, until the guard wandered away.

Now, said the voice.

She kept climbing until she came to a

narrow window about halfway up, then squeezed through and into a corridor, landing in a crouch. No one was around. Faint torchlight flickered at one end, and a solid wooden door blocked the other.

She removed her cloak and tucked it into her backpack. The girl was small and thin with silver-blond hair and a pinched, serious face. The dark colors she wore were mottled like shadows. She crept toward the door and listened for a moment, then slowly lifted the latch and entered.

Beyond were more corridors, some dark, some lit by torchlight. She moved cautiously. At one point, she stopped and sank into the shadows as a servant scurried past. The floor had rich red carpet now, and torches burned in alcoves.

On the left, said the voice.

The girl paused. The patch of wall to her left seemed different, the stonework slightly pale. She felt around the edges until she was sure, then pushed at one stone.

The wall swung inward, revealing a hidden entrance.

The girl's expression didn't change. She tiptoed into the darkness along a narrow passage, feeling her way until she reached another door, opened it, and entered a room.

Inside it was bright with lamplight. Every inch shone with precious metal, dark polished wood, and crystal. Beautiful embroideries covered the walls, shimmering with golden thread. In the middle of the room sat a huge four-poster bed.

This is it, said the voice. *King Godfic's royal quarters!*

The girl stared around, her mouth open.

Come on. We'd better be quick.

She nodded and tiptoed across to a grand dressing table in front of an enormous mirror.

He likes looking at himself, doesn't he?

The girl grinned and checked the drawers. One was full of little jars of powder and perfume. One held a display of embroidered lace handkerchiefs. One had papers and wax and the king's official stamp.

One was locked. The girl pulled two pins

from her hair and carefully used them to feel inside the lock. Then she *twisted*, and the lock clicked. She slid the drawer open and gasped.

The inside was lined with dark-red velvet, and its contents glittered. There were gold and silver rings, a heavy gold link necklace, and a chain of pearls. Beautiful, ornate pins were carved into the shapes of animals, inlaid with precious stones. Coins lay scattered at the base. And in the center, on its own stand, sat a large golden brooch with a grand diamond.

That's it!

Carefully, the girl picked up the brooch and examined it. The base was an octagon, with eight ornate golden sides, framing a diamond that shone like a star. There was something in the diamond's heart—or perhaps it was painted underneath? Peering closer at the diamond, she made out an eye, beautifully drawn, fierce, and somehow cruel. Not a human eye; more like a cat's, or a wolf's, or . . .

I don't like that.

"What?" The girl was surprised. "It's just a picture."

It's creepy.

She shrugged and looked back—and the eye moved.

"Argh!" she yelled, dropping the brooch to the floor. The eye glanced around, then straight at her, and blinked! Suddenly a bell started tolling from the corridor outside, hard and fast and sharp.

You've triggered an alarm!

"It moved!" she hissed.

I know! Forget it! Come on!

There were other noises now, shouts and running footsteps. The girl ran back to the far wall and the secret passage, closing the door behind her just as she heard someone at the main entrance.

She fumbled through the black corridor, trying to stay quiet. Would they know about the hidden entry? She reached the end of the passage and pushed the door open a crack. The corridor was empty, and she hurried back to where she'd come in, dragging her cloak and a grappling rope from her bag. She poked her head through the slit window, then pulled it back sharply and cursed. There were guards all along the top of the wall now, holding lanterns and searching intently.

We can't go that way—they'll see us!

The girl felt panic rise inside her. "Maybe—"

Boots thundered behind her. More guards!

DRAGON STORM

She raced toward the brighter end of the corridor, back into the depths of the palace.

What are we going to do?

She kept moving, glancing around. There were rooms on either side. Could she sneak into one of them? The alarm bells clanged, and a guard shouted, "You check that way!"

What are we going to DO, Cara?

And then a black-gloved hand reached from a doorway, covered her mouth, and dragged her backward. The door closed behind her, and someone grabbed her arms and whispered harshly in her ear.

2
STREET RAT

"Be quiet."

It was a man's voice, and he was strong, pinning down Cara's arms. *"Don't move."*

Cara snorted. She lifted her feet and slammed both heels *hard* against the side of one kneecap. The man cursed and half collapsed. Cara pulled away from him and reached for the door.

"Wait!"

At the last moment she heard boots in the corridor. *Guards!* She looked back at the man, now clutching his knee in pain. He held a finger to his lips. "Shh!"

Cara hesitated and waited for the footsteps to fade away.

The man nodded. "It was the tower watch," he said. "They always come this way. They're looking for you."

He was young, dressed in dark clothes, with curly black hair and a friendly expression. An old, faded scar marked one side of his face. Cara glanced around warily. They were in a small room, simple but clean. A thin bed rested against one wall, and a table and chair were at the other, with several lit candles, an inkwell, long feather pens, and neat piles of paper on the table.

The man stood, wincing and rubbing his knee. "Good move, by the way. Daisy would be impressed." He held out a hand. "I'm Malik."

Cara didn't know who Daisy was. She ignored him and turned back to the door.

"You won't be able to climb down the wall, you know."

She stopped.

"I saw you climb up," he said. "Very impressive! But they're watching now; they'll see you if you try to get down that way."

Cara knew he was right. What was she going to do?

"I know another way," he said. "I can get you out."

She scowled. "Why would I trust you?"

Malik shrugged. "I could have shouted for the guards. You're a street rat, aren't you?"

She didn't answer.

He nodded. "No parents. Nowhere to live. Surviving on the streets and on your wits. That was me once. I was like you. I admit, I stole an apple when I had to." Then he laughed. "Nothing like this, though! What on earth were you looking for, sneaking into the palace?"

Cara said nothing, but he didn't seem to mind. "These days I do something different," he said.

Cara looked again at the quills and paper. "A clerk."

"Yes . . . but something else too. I look for people." His voice changed. Suddenly he seemed more serious. "Special people. Ones who see things others don't. A face in the fire, maybe?"

Cara frowned. What was he talking about?

We should go, said the voice in her head.

She nodded and reached for the door handle.

"Or perhaps hear things?" called Malik.

Cara stopped and looked back. "What?"

Malik nodded. "People who hear things others can't," he said quietly. "Like a voice, always there, that knows things you don't. A voice that helps you."

How can he know that, Cara?

Cara shook her head.

Malik smiled. "As soon as I saw you, I could tell. It's like a *glow,* you know?" She said nothing. "Would you like to know what it is?"

Slowly, Cara released the handle. The corridor outside was empty. She knew she should go, but she wanted to hear what Malik would say next.

"Would you like to see whose voice it is?" asked Malik.

What's he talking about, Cara? What does he mean, "whose voice"?

Cara chewed her lip. Then she gave a very short nod.

Malik grinned. "Great! Um . . ." He picked up one of the lit candles. "Right. I'm not very good at this, but I can show you for a moment. Watch the flame."

Warily, Cara watched it, flickering and glowing. It seemed quite normal.

The man moved his other hand in a complex pattern, muttering.

I don't like this, said the voice. *He's trying to trick you!*

But Cara watched the flame, and it stretched, filling the room with warm yellow light. And within it, she realized that she could see something. A face with a soft chin and glowing eyes. It was familiar somehow.

"There," whispered Malik.

Cara glanced up and jumped! There, against the wall, faint as a ghost, stood a creature with long ears, a catlike face, and glowing green eyes. The body was hard to make out because it seemed to shift and change color. Cara stepped back, ready to run! But the face . . .

"Is that—" She stopped. "Is that *you*?"

"I don't know," said the voice. And Cara gasped. It wasn't in her head anymore—that voice was coming from the creature! It stared down at itself and then back at Cara.

It held up one claw, pale and ghostly.

"What is this?" it said, astonished. "What's going on?"

"I can't bring her completely into this world," said Malik. "You'll need Drun's help for that. But this is what she looks like."

The creature gazed into Cara's face.

"Cara, I think this is . . . I think this is *me*! I think . . ." It stopped. "*Silverthief*," she murmured. "That's my name. *Silverthief.* Cara, I think I'm a—"

And then a fist hammered against the door, and an angry voice shouted, "Open up in there! Open this door in the name of the king!"

3

THE GUILD

"Open up!"

Cara gasped and stared at the door. Behind her, Malik blew out the candle. "Sorry, Silverthief," he muttered. Cara turned back to see the creature's image fading away like smoke.

"Cara, what's happening?" she hissed, and then she was gone—but a moment later Cara heard the familiar voice in her mind.

Cara! That was me! I think that was me!

Cara shook her head and tried to focus. How could she escape? The tiny slit window in this room was too small, and there was nowhere to hide.

Malik walked toward the door. "Coming!"

"No!" hissed Cara, but he winked and reached for the handle. At the last moment, Cara flattened herself against the wall behind the door as Malik swung it open wide.

"Captain Hork!" he said, beaming.

Cara tried not to breathe. She peered through the gap between the door hinge and the wall. She saw a group of soldiers. Among them was a large man with badly fitting bronze armor and a ridiculous plumed helmet. Cara knew

Captain Hork. He was
captain of the King's
Guard, a bully and
a fool. Her heart
pounded.

"What can I do for
you?" asked Malik.

Captain Hork gaped.
"Don't you hear the alarm?" he snarled. "The
king's been robbed! Have you seen anyone
acting suspiciously?"

"Gosh," said Malik, looking shocked. "How
awful! No, sorry. But . . . someone *did* just
run past my door. Someone big and fierce, it
sounded like! He went that way." He pointed
down the corridor.

"Right," snapped Hork, adjusting his helmet. "Next time, pay a bit more attention, eh? The king's life could be at stake!"

He paused and seemed to think. "Big and fierce, you say?"

Malik nodded. *"Very."*

"Hmm. Right. Um . . . lead on, men! I'll, um, guard the rear."

The soldiers ran off with Captain Hork bellowing after them and keeping a safe distance behind.

Malik waited until Hork's voice faded and then closed the door. "That should keep them busy," he chuckled.

Cara breathed out. She glanced at the corner of the room, but the strange creature had vanished. "Where did she go?" she asked.

"Back to her world," said Malik. "Drun can help you bring her back."

"Who's Drun?"

"A friend of mine. I'd like you to meet him. And some other friends too. People who know what it's like to be special."

He looked serious now. "Would you like to meet them?"

Cara, I think that really was me! I think . . .

Cara hesitated. "All right." She frowned. "But what was it? That creature?"

Malik smiled. "I think you've already guessed," he said. "Tell me . . . what do you know about dragons?"

Malik found an apprentice cloak for Cara and walked her out of the palace as his new assistant, loudly giving her instructions whenever they passed a guard. Dawn was breaking. As they came down from the rock and into the city, a few people were moving around. They were setting up stalls or carting fish ready for the day's markets.

"This way," murmured Malik, steering her down an alley. Cara recognized where they were and felt her skin prickle. This was the Vennels, a dangerous part of town and one she normally stayed clear of. She checked that she still had her knife tucked into one boot.

CARA AND SILVERTHIEF

What do you know about dragons?

Cara thought about this. She knew what everyone knew. That they were ferocious and terrifying. That they destroyed crops and attacked humans. And that they were a *myth*—a made-up story of monsters that might have existed a thousand years ago, but not today. Not here.

Oh, there were stories. Cara kept to herself mostly. But sometimes, when the rain was lashing and the wind howling, she would huddle for shelter with some of the other street rats, and someone would always make wild claims: *My mate says he saw something flying over the West Gate. I saw something moving, and it weren't human! There was a light, not natural. Magic, I*

29

reckon. But it was all nonsense. There were no dragons. There was no magic.

But . . . the eye in the jewel had moved; she was sure of it. And then there was that creature in Malik's room. And the voice in her mind that had always been there, for so long she had never even thought about it.

"Not everyone can see them or hear them," said Malik. "They live in their own world. But some of us—*dragonseers*—can connect. We can see them, hear them, talk to them. We can even summon them into this world."

"And that's what we saw? That's what you were showing me—my . . . my *dragon*?"

Malik chuckled. "Oh, yes."

He ducked down into a tiny lane between two collapsed houses, and Cara tried to keep up.

"But people would *know*," she tried. "I mean, *dragons*?"

"Well, there aren't very many these days. For centuries there were none at all, after the Dragon Storm."

"I remember that story," said Cara. "That was the war, wasn't it? Between humans and dragons. And we won, and the dragons ran away."

Malik sighed. "My goodness, what do they teach kids these days? No. It wasn't between humans and dragons, we didn't win, and they didn't run away. They just . . . left." He grimaced. "To be honest, I think they were disappointed with us."

He shook his head. "But now they're coming back. It's very exciting! A new generation of dragons—and a new generation of *dragonseers*. Like you." He stopped at a plain-looking door on an old cottage. "Ah, here we are!"

Beyond the plain-looking door was another door, which opened into a long, snaking corridor. And then there was a maze of twisting passages and false doorways. The cottage was far larger than it had appeared from the outside. Cara tried to work out where they were, but everything looked the same. She felt a strange movement under her feet and heard the sound of gears whirring. She realized that the corridors were moving and turning as they walked.

Finally they reached a larger doorway, and Malik paused. "Ready?" he asked. His eyes twinkled mischievously.

Cara frowned. "For what?"

Malik grinned. "For this!"

In one smooth movement he swung open the door and steered her through. "Welcome to the Dragonseer Guild!"

Cara stared in astonishment. "No *way*," she managed at last.

4
DRAGONSEER

They were standing on a raised platform, at the edge of an enormous cavern that stretched far off into the distance. Below them were buildings and what looked like a training ground. The air was full of strange globes that hung from the ceiling and shone pale yellow like the early-morning sun. It was the largest place Cara had ever seen. It was *colossal*.

"This is impossible," she gasped. "There's

nowhere in the city big enough for this. Where *are* we? Are we underground?"

Malik just grinned. "Come on. Let's meet the others."

He led her down to the ground and toward a collection of huts. Cara tried not to stare as she walked through the hall. There were other people, she realized. From a training area on one side came the sounds of laughter, shouting, and the clash of metal swords. A tall man in a shabby gray cloak stalked past them, nodding briefly to Malik and ignoring Cara completely. She could smell woodsmoke and breakfast.

They reached the huts, and Malik asked her to wait as he slipped inside one.

Cara gazed around.

CARA AND SILVERTHIEF

What is all this, Cara?

The voice in her head felt like a comfort.

"I don't know," she whispered.

Malik returned with a woman, tall and kindly-looking, dressed in blue robes. She nodded to Cara. "Welcome, Cara," she said. "My name is Berin. Malik has told me about you and Silverthief. I'm sure you have questions, and we'll try to answer them all. But for now . . . this is the Guild!" She gave a great warm smile, and Cara found it hard not to smile back.

"So . . . ," Cara started to say, but stopped. "It's true, then? I'm a . . . a dragonseer?"

37

It sounded ridiculous. But Berin smiled again.

"Oh, yes. Malik is always right about these things," she said. "You're a dragonseer. Silverthief is your dragon, and you are her human. There *are* dragons, Cara. There *is* dragon magic. It's all true."

"And the voice in my head . . . all this time, it was . . . *her?*"

Cara couldn't remember her parents. She'd been living on the streets of Rivven for so long she couldn't remember anything from before. Her days were cold, hungry, and dangerous. All she had was the mysterious voice—the voice that knew how to find hidden things. A voice that knew things Cara couldn't possibly have known herself. Together they had learned how to get by, how to find shelter, how to stay alive. The voice had been with her for so long that she'd never even questioned it.

"It happens sometimes," said Berin. "At some point, you connected with Silverthief, but you were so young you didn't know what you'd done, and neither did she. She's stayed with you. You two are closer than any dragon pair we've ever met."

Cara nodded. "So what do you want from me?" she asked warily.

Berin laughed. "Nothing! The Guild is here for *you*. We can teach you how to summon Silverthief and protect her. And we can offer you a family, in a way. You can be one of us, if you'd like."

Cara hesitated.

I don't know, said the voice—Silverthief's voice. *We've done all right by ourselves, Cara.*

"I can . . . summon her? Make her real?" Cara asked. Berin nodded. "And would I still hear her voice?"

Berin smiled. "Of course!"

"And I can leave when I like?"

"Yes."

Cara squinted at Berin and then Malik. He nodded encouragingly.

She bit her lip. "All right. For now."

Berin clapped her hands. "Excellent! We'll get you settled, show you where your dorm room is, and introduce you to some of the other children. But first . . ." She studied Cara. "First, there's someone I'd like you to meet. Come with me."

She brought Cara to a round building away from the other huts and introduced her to a short, cheerful man who turned out to be Drun. He was dressed in a brown leather jerkin and pants and had a wild gray beard.

"It's a pleasure to meet you!" he said, shaking her hand. He gazed at her face and nodded. "Oh, yes. You've got the look all right. Come on in."

Dragon Storm

Drun led Cara to a smoky fire and told her to look into the flames.

Cara was wary. The building was dark and full of shadows cast by the fire. She wasn't sure how to get out if she needed to. But she looked into the flames as Drun muttered, and the flames rose.

"Tell me about Silverthief," he murmured. "What does she look like?"

Cara frowned. "Don't they all look the same?"

But Drun laughed. "Oh, no. Dragons are special, miss. Every one is unique. It depends on the human, you see. They all look different, they all have different abilities, and they'll all get their different powers eventually."

"Powers?"

"Oh, yes," Drun answered. "Each dragon's got one. A *special* power. One that only appears when it's most needed."

Cara described Silverthief, and the flames rose higher again, crackling and sparking suddenly, and she felt goose bumps on her arms.

Then Silverthief appeared.

For real this time: solid, not faint and ghostly. A real creature, with silvery skin and short teeth, oval green eyes, and a careful, watchful face. Silverthief looked down at her body and then up at Cara, and tentatively reached out.

Cara reached back. "Silverthief?"

They touched. Real. She was *real*. Cara could feel her rough, strong claws against her fingertips! She felt a shiver of excitement, and Silverthief smiled, half closed her eyes like a happy cat, and purred.

"Hello, Cara."

5
THE NORTH RUINS

Cara still couldn't figure out where the Dragonseer Guild Hall was, or how anything so large could exist in Rivven. She knew it was old—ancient, even. The training ground and huts were new, but beyond them lay the ruins of older buildings from a different age.

She'd been at the Guild for a few days, enough time to learn a lot about it. Now she sat atop one of the ruined walls with

Silverthief curled around her, and wondered about her new life.

That first day, the day Cara had summoned Silverthief, Drun had told her the rules.

"Silverthief can't stay forever," he'd said. "She needs your connection to keep her in this world, so when you sleep, she goes back. But I bet you'll have no problem calling her again. Good luck!"

Berin had shown Cara around the rest of the hall, the dorm rooms, and the central hut where they met for meals and lessons. Then Berin had introduced Cara to the other children.

There was Connor, who was clever and a bit of a show-off. Mira was obsessed with

devices and machines and was often grease-
smudged. Erin was a tall, strong girl who
strode everywhere and shouted a lot. Kai was
quiet and studied everything he could about
dragon biology. And Ellis was the explorer,
constantly making maps. They'd all been
friendly to her, but Cara wasn't used to other
people and found them a little overwhelming.

She'd also met the other dragons and
found that Silverthief was small, compared
with them. Rockhammer, Erin's dragon,
was almost twice as big, and only Connor's
strange, whiplike creature, Lightspirit, was
smaller than Silverthief.

Cara didn't care about the other dragons,
though. Some of the other children found

summoning hard, but for Cara, creating the doorway that allowed Silverthief into her world was as easy as breathing. The voice in her head had been her only friend for years, and now her friend was real.

Life in the Guild was good—regular food, real beds, no danger. It was perfect.

Almost perfect . . .

"I don't trust them."

Cara patted Silverthief's smooth, warm sides.

"I know," Cara said. "But they've been good to us so far."

The dragon snorted. "So far. What do they *really* want? What aren't they telling us?"

"Like what?" asked Cara, frowning.

"Like . . ." Silverthief flicked her tail. "Like where this place *is*."

Cara shrugged. "I suppose they want to keep it safe."

"Hmph. And I don't like the other dragons."

Cara smiled. "I know, Silver."

"Rockhammer is *so* annoying. He's always bellowing! And Boneshadow's boring. And they keep wanting to *talk* to me." Silverthief sighed. "It was always just you and me before. I don't like it now."

Cara laughed. "You love being a dragon," she said. "And you like it when I scratch behind your ears."

"Well . . ." Silverthief stretched her neck, purring as Cara scratched. "Well, yes."

Cara patted her again. Silverthief's skin was faintly silver, but her colors shimmered and changed to match wherever she was, similar to a chameleon. Like Cara, Silverthief had the knack of keeping very, very still, until she almost disappeared.

"Cara!"

Cara looked down. Heading toward them were two of the other children, Ellis and Mira, and their dragons.

"Don't answer them," hissed Silverthief, but Cara shushed her.

"What?"

"We're going exploring!" called Ellis. He

held up a piece of parchment, his latest map. "The ruins at the north end. Want to come?"

Cara gazed down, thinking.

Ellis was okay. He loved mapmaking, and since Cara enjoyed poking around and exploring, they got along well. She wasn't sure about Mira. They shared a dorm room, but Mira asked hundreds of questions, and Cara liked to keep to herself. They didn't talk much. Now she waited politely. Cara suspected Mira didn't really want her to come along.

"Um . . ."

"Come on!" shouted Ellis. "It'll be fun!" He grinned up at her, and she smiled despite herself.

"Okay."

DRAGON STORM

She leaped down from the roof. Silverthief followed. Ellis's dragon, Pathseeker, was sturdy and not much larger than Silverthief. They greeted each other with a friendly sniff. Flameteller, Mira's dragon, pattered back a few steps. He was nervous a lot, and cautious around Silverthief.

"Where to?" asked Cara.

Ellis led them northward. "I found some entrances," he said. "I think there are caves underneath this one! I marked them down." He waved his map.

"Ellis said Silverthief is good at finding hidden things," said Mira. "Is that right?"

Cara hesitated and then gave a curt nod.

Mira beamed. "Great! She can help us. And I've invented something!" She held up a strange gadget with a cable and a lantern. "It's so we can send down a light to check. In case we come across any holes." She pushed it toward Cara. "See? We can move it up and down with this handle!"

Cara shrugged. Mira was fine, she supposed, but her enthusiasm was sometimes very draining.

Silverthief gave a loud, exaggerated sigh, and Mira stopped and looked embarrassed.

Cara tried not to giggle.

Ellis led them through the ruins at the edge of the hall. It was darker here, away from the globes. The ground was thick with weeds and twisted thornbushes and the remains of ancient streets. Collapsed buildings lay slumped around them.

Cara felt Silverthief tremble with excitement, and grinned. It felt like something new and hidden.

"There!" murmured Ellis.

Tucked half into one of the mounds was an entrance—a dark square gap that led underground. It looked inviting, but as they got nearer, Ellis groaned. A rope was stretched in front of the entrance, and hanging from it was a sign, which read:

THIS AREA IS OUT-OF-BOUNDS FOR SAFETY REASONS

DO NOT ENTER

Vice Chancellor Creedy

"Rats," said Mira.

Cara scowled. Vice Chancellor Creedy was Berin's second-in-command. He was a grim-faced man who taught them dragon riding, and always looked at the children as if there was a bad taste in his mouth.

Silverthief hissed quietly, *"See?"*

Cara frowned. "See what?"

"They're keeping *secrets*," muttered the dragon. "What's down there? What don't they want us to see?"

"It's just for safety," said Cara, but Silverthief shook her head.

"No, there's something hidden down there. I can *smell* it."

Ellis sighed in frustration. "Well . . . I guess that's that."

Cara considered it. "We could go in anyway," she said. "We've got the dragons."

"But the sign says not to," said Mira.

Cara shrugged. "Creedy isn't here—he'll never know, right? Don't you want to see what's down there?"

"Maybe just a *few* steps . . . ," said Ellis doubtfully.

But Mira shook her head. "No, we shouldn't!"

Cara snorted. "Do what you want. *I'm* going in."

She lifted the rope and stepped underneath. Silverthief followed her, and after a moment so did Ellis and Pathseeker, leaving Mira behind. Cara peered into the darkness and felt a familiar excitement. Silverthief was right; there were secrets down there. And together, Cara and Silverthief would sniff them out. . . .

"All right," she said. "Let's *explore*."

6
EXPLORING

Beyond the entrance, a set of worn stone steps led down into darkness. Pathseeker crept down first, sniffing carefully. Ellis took another lantern from his backpack, lit the candle, and held it up. Cara and Silverthief followed.

The air was cool and smelled of ancient dead leaves. At the bottom of the steps, they walked along a corridor that turned sharp left after a few yards. The outside light was lost. Darkness crowded in. The pale circle of light from the lanterns made shadows jump and swing as they moved.

"These are really old," whispered Ellis, looking at the walls. They were covered in carvings: scenes from battles, images of humans and dragons building something. "I think . . . *thousands* of years old."

The corridor was long and turned often, rising and falling. Ellis gave Cara the lamp and pulled out more paper. He drew the tunnels as they walked. Ahead of him, Pathseeker muttered things like "North by northwest, twenty-five yards, on a one-sixteenth incline," and Ellis scribbled notes. After a while they came to a junction, and the tunnel split into two. Ellis peered down both routes.

"Which way?"

"Left," said Silverthief without hesitating. "I can feel something hidden."

Ellis grinned and turned left. Three more times the corridor split, and each time Silverthief gave directions. Cara studied the images on the walls as they passed: a lightning bolt, a dragon's wing spread out, a tower, a huge creature with glowing eyes staring down at a crowd of people, a crown, and an army going to war.

"Where are we?" she asked.

Ellis peered at his map. "According to this . . . near the middle of the Guild Hall. But much farther down."

"Stop," said Pathseeker suddenly. The dragonseers looked up, and Cara raised her lamp. Ahead of them, the corridor ended. There was the shape of a doorway but no door within it—just more solid stone wall. There was no keyhole, no door handle. No way through.

"Silver?" asked Cara.

Silverthief came to the front and snuffled around the doorframe. "There's a way through," she muttered. "I can *feel* it. But . . ."

Ellis and Pathseeker waited. Then Cara

felt something: a faint draft, like a prickle up the back of her neck. The lamplight seemed to dim. She lifted the lamp, checking the candle, and noticed that above the stone doorway, there was an eye.

It was carved into an octagon, like the base of the brooch in the king's room. It had the same fierce aspect. Before, she'd thought it might be from a cat or a wolf. Now she knew it was from a dragon. But not like Silverthief. This was something cruel, glaring out from the rock. Cara stared at it, her hand trembling, waiting for it to move. . . .

"What are you doing here?" barked a voice.

Ellis and Cara jumped. They spun around, and the lamp cast wild shadows against the walls. A brilliant yellow light suddenly blinded them.

Pathseeker staggered and shook her head. Silverthief shimmered into the same color and pattern as the stone behind her.

The light moved, and Cara reached for her boot knife.

But it was Vice Chancellor Creedy who strode forward and glared at them.

His staff glowed a sick yellow, and it shone against his pale, sour face. He looked furious. "This area is out-of-bounds!" he snapped. "What do you think you're doing?"

The children stared at him, their hearts pounding. At last Ellis said, "Exploring?"

"There was a clear sign!" snapped Creedy.

"The tunnels are forbidden for *safety* reasons. Leave this area immediately!" He jabbed a finger back down the corridor. Ellis and Pathseeker meekly headed back.

Silverthief hissed, and Cara lifted her chin. "What safety reasons?"

Creedy gave her a look of contempt. "These are ancient ruins, *girl,*" he growled. "The tunnels could collapse at any moment! Are you a fool?"

She held his gaze for a few seconds. Creedy glared back at her. Eventually Cara nodded and followed Ellis back up the corridor.

Silverthief hissed again.

Creedy herded them back to the hut like an angry shepherd driving lost sheep. He muttered to himself about foolish children the entire way.

When they arrived, Berin was waiting for them. Her face was stern but not angry. Next to her, and desperately trying to shrink into the background, was Mira.

"Hello, children," said Berin. "I'm glad you're safe."

Cara said nothing. She glared at Mira, who squirmed.

Berin lifted her hands. "It's not Mira's fault. She did the right thing. She was worried about you." She raised one eyebrow. "After all, you entered an area specifically marked as dangerous."

"We were being careful—" started Ellis.

"It was perfectly safe!" snapped Cara. "There was nothing wrong down there!"

Berin remained calm. "The tunnels are ancient, Cara, and have been unmapped for centuries. Until we've investigated them, we won't know what state they're in, or where a wrong turn might have led you. Trust us on this, hmm?"

She smiled, but Cara looked away.

"Ellis," continued Berin, "I've warned you about your wandering. Exploring is a fine calling, but keep to safe areas, all right?"

He nodded.

"Good," said Berin. "Off you go."

Ellis and Mira scurried away. But as Cara turned, Berin said, "Not you, Cara. You and I need to talk."

7
TRUST
NO ONE

Berin waited until the others had left and then pulled out a chair. "Would you like to sit?"

Cara shook her head.

Berin smiled. "No, you like to be on your feet, don't you? Always ready to run away."

Cara said nothing. Berlin was right. Cara didn't like to feel trapped, or to have her back to doorways.

Berin sat down herself and looked up. "So," she said brightly. "Tell me, Cara. How are things?"

Cara frowned. "What do you mean?"

"Well . . ." Berin waved an arm vaguely. "Are you enjoying life in the Guild? Lessons?"

"S'pose," admitted Cara. "Better than living on the streets."

Berin chuckled. "I imagine! And there's Silverthief, of course. How are things with her? You seem very close."

Cara nodded.

Berin seemed to hesitate. "It's just . . . I was wondering if you felt you were settling in. I know it's a big change, but the Guild is here for you. *We're* here for you. Are you making friends?"

Cara shrugged. "Ellis is okay."

"And the others?"

Cara said nothing. She didn't understand what Berin wanted her to say. She didn't mind the others. She didn't need them either. She had Silverthief.

"We'd like you to feel settled."

Cara frowned again. "You said I could leave when I wanted."

"Well, yes," said Berin, surprised. "But I'd hoped . . ." She looked at Cara for a few moments longer. Eventually she gave an apologetic smile. "Well. If you want to talk,

I'm here, anytime. For now please stay within the safe areas. And . . . try to relax." She smiled. "You're safe here, you know."

Cara nodded. Then she turned and left.

It was the weekend, and many of the children had gone home to see parents or friends. Mira, Ellis, and Cara were the only children still there. Dinner was quiet. Mira tried starting a conversation, but Cara ignored her. Ellis was distracted with updating his maps.

That evening, lying in bed, Cara talked to Silverthief.

"I can't believe Mira ratted us out," she

whispered, so quietly she hardly even breathed the words.

I know! replied Silverthief at once. She spoke to Cara in her head, as she had before. *And what was Berin talking about? "Are you making friends?" What's it got to do with her?*

Cara nodded.

And there's something else, said Silverthief. *They're hiding something. I'm sure of it.*

Cara frowned. "What?"

Think about it. All those branching tunnels, all those junctions we took. It was like a maze down there, wasn't it?

"So?"

So . . . how did Creedy find us so quickly?

Cara blinked. It was true. Mira must have

gone back to the Guild to tell Creedy, and he would have had to follow the exact same path that they'd taken in order to find them so quickly.

"Maybe he heard us?"

Silverthief snorted. *And I saw something else too.*

"What?"

Footprints. There were footprints in the sand, Cara. Someone had been down before us. They went right up to that door . . . and through it.

Cara stared at the ceiling, thinking.

We can't trust them, said Silverthief. *There's something they're not telling us. And it's on the other side of that door.*

For the next few days, Cara just watched.

Nothing seemed different. The other children returned, bubbling with excitement and stories and eager to see their dragons again (summoning outside the Guild Hall was strictly forbidden). Creedy continued the riding and flying lessons, wearing his usual scowl. Drun taught them more about summoning and dragon care. And Daisy, the short self-defense teacher, trained them in techniques for evading and escaping capture. She was impressed by Cara, and often made her demonstrate to the others, much to Cara's embarrassment.

Cara watched the other children as they talked and laughed, argued and joked. It was strange, the way they went on. It seemed so easy. She wondered what it would be like to join in, but couldn't think of what to say.

Another boy joined the group, a blacksmith's son called Tomás, and Cara saw how quickly he settled in. She wondered why she found it so hard. Occasionally someone smiled at her, or seemed to be on the edge of inviting her to join them.

Ugh, no, said Silverthief. *They're so annoying!*

It was true. Erin was the worst, with her huge, booming laugh, always trying to take over the conversation.

And Connor thinks he's so clever, sneered Silverthief. *And Kai's always asking me about my camouflage; he's really nosy.*

78

Cara nodded. Silverthief was right, of course. But . . . Ellis was nice. Exploring had been . . . fun? She wondered if she should tell him about Creedy.

We can't trust him. He'll just tell a grown-up, like Mira did.

Cara wasn't sure about that, but Silverthief's voice was firm.

We can't trust any of them, Cara. There's just us. We have to solve this together.

In the evenings she didn't join in the conversations with Erin and Mira. She just sat on her bunk with her back against the wall, completely still, as she used to when she was on the streets. She sat until she seemed to fade away, until the others stopped noticing her, stopped even thinking about her. At night, when the others slept, she crept up onto the roof and watched the hall, enjoying the silence. Occasionally she saw people moving around. But they didn't see her.

One time, she saw Tomás leave. He looked sad, and she wondered if, perhaps, he'd also found it hard to fit in. Silverthief told her that Tom couldn't hold the connection with his own dragon, Ironskin.

That means he's not a proper dragonseer, she said rather gleefully.

But a few days later, he returned and seemed much happier, and suddenly Ironskin could stay with him for as long as she wanted. *And* Ironskin had developed her first special power—Protection magic—and she was now able to create a shield around herself and others. Cara didn't know what had happened and felt too awkward to ask. She wondered what Silverthief's powers would be.

Often, Cara noticed Creedy moving around. He would creep out of the Guild Hall and return an hour later, or more. Sometimes Cara fell asleep before he returned. She wondered what he was up to.

One evening, he didn't go outside. Instead he peered around carefully, and then strode northward toward the ruins and the entrance Ellis had discovered.

Cara slipped silently down from the roof and followed him.

8
SECRETS

The world was dark. The globes that hung from the ceiling were now as dim and faint as stars. Everything was shadow. Cara followed Vice Chancellor Creedy as he hurried toward the north end of the hall and the entrance that led underground.

Creedy slipped under the warning rope and down the steps. Cara crept closer and peered inside. As she did, a faint yellow light appeared, and she saw Creedy's face in the glow of his staff. His expression was serious.

I knew it! hissed Silverthief in her mind.

Cara nodded and slunk down the steps after him.

She had no lamp or matches—and wouldn't have dared to light them anyway—but her night vision was good. Carefully, staying just behind the light, she followed Creedy. At each split in the tunnels, he turned without stopping. Silverthief had been right, she realized. Creedy knew exactly where he was going.

At the last turning, Cara paused. She could hear something from around the corner—

a faint scraping sound. She took a deep breath and poked her head out.

The vice chancellor was standing at the stone wall that Cara and Ellis had reached before. He seemed to be drawing a pattern on the wall in chalk. The pattern was complex and twirling, and at its heart was an eye inside an octagon.

He muttered as he drew. Then he finished, put the chalk away, and pressed against the shape of the door.

The door slid open.

A magic lock, murmured Silverthief. *That's why I couldn't find it!*

Creedy stepped through, and a few seconds later Cara followed him. The hallway beyond had walls of smooth white stone and white sand underfoot. A dim red light came from another doorway at the far end. Creedy must have gone that way. Cara crept forward and peered inside.

It was a wide, tall chamber. The ceiling was covered in jewels that glowed with the strange red light. At the far wall there was another doorway, perhaps leading to more passages. Inside she could see a sarcophagus, an ancient stone coffin. Standing on top

was a statue of a woman with a powerful expression.

Creedy was standing next to the coffin. He was closer than she'd expected—if he turned his head a fraction, he would see her! Cara froze, but she didn't gasp. She didn't make any sound at all. She concentrated on breathing silently, and tried to let herself become invisible.

Creedy didn't notice her. He was looking up at something Cara couldn't see. He seemed nervous, she thought, and his face was pale.

"You must understand," he said. "The importance of this—"

There was a reply, low and fierce.

"*Let. Me. Go.*"

There was someone else in the room! The voice was old and tired, but burned with anger.

Creedy shook his head. "You know the deal. If you want me to set you free, give me the jewel."

"But it's *mine!*"

Set you free? wondered Cara. Who was this person? Was Creedy keeping them *prisoner?* She strained forward, trying to see. She could make out faint lines in the air, like a barrier. The lines were pale yellow, and they fizzed with a sound like a crackling fire. Cara stretched a little farther.

Sand scrunched under her foot, and Creedy turned. Cara pulled back like a snake.

"Hello?" called Creedy sharply.

Oh, no! whispered Silverthief's voice. *Go now, Cara!*

Cara crept back up the corridor, trying to move quickly and silently.

"Is someone there?"

Creedy's voice was closer now. He was coming! She turned and raced away, the sand tugging at her feet. Around the corner, and the next, into almost pitch-black, she ran. Behind her, Cara heard footsteps and saw yellow light swing to and fro as the vice chancellor ran up the hallway after her.

"Show yourself!" he bellowed. "Who are you? Stop!"

9

A PLAN

Cara raced through the stone doorway and down the corridor, bouncing against the walls in the darkness. Creedy had the light from his staff to guide him, and he was gaining on her. She reached a junction, and another, scrambling to get out. But then she realized: even if she made it to the entrance, he would see her. What could she do?

She skidded to a halt.

What are you doing? came Silverthief's voice.

Cara ignored her and backed up to the last junction. Then she tiptoed a few steps up the other path and crouched low in the darkness. The light came nearer, and she watched as Creedy hurried past and toward the entrance.

She heard his feet pounding, and then silence. She waited in the dark, not daring to move. Had he really left? Or was he waiting for her? Would he come back? But at last she peeked out to the junction and listened. Nothing.

She checked the stone doorway, but it was closed again. The vice chancellor must have shut it behind him as he chased her.

She summoned Silverthief, and the little dragon snuffled around the frame. "No," she said at last. "It's magic, Cara. I can't get through this."

Cara nodded, and they made their way to the entrance. She listened again, but Creedy wasn't there. He must have run all the way back to the Guild buildings, looking for her. She breathed a sigh of relief, left the tunnels, and walked back to the dorm. As she got into bed, the globes were already starting to glow brighter, creating a fake dawn.

Her mind raced. Who was the prisoner? What was the jewel Creedy wanted? Had he seen her? Whom could she tell?

No one, whispered Silverthief. *We can't trust anyone.*

Cara fell into an uneasy sleep. She woke up an hour later, tired and confused. It was another morning.

Vice Chancellor Creedy was lying. He'd told the children that the tunnels were closed for safety reasons, but that wasn't it at all. He was keeping someone prisoner, and demanding something in return for letting them go. Did Berin know too?

She must, said Silverthief. *Creedy is her second-in-command!*

"Who can we tell, then?"

No one.

Drun was teaching them dragon care that day. All the dragons were there. Huge Rockhammer was bending over Erin; wily Lightspirit was talking with Connor; Ellis was with the odd, stumpy Pathseeker. Mira was there with Flameteller, the strange angular creature who looked almost like a model of bronze and wood, and Tom with Ironskin, her dark-red skin streaked in orange and yellow lines of fire. Kai was stroking Boneshadow, the white dragon with a red flare on her chest.

Ellis gave Cara a friendly wave, and she nodded.

"Maybe we could tell the others," she whispered.

Ha! said Silverthief scornfully. *Like Mira? She'd just tell the adults!*

"Ellis?"

Silverthief said nothing. *Perhaps Ellis,* thought Cara. *Tom seems all right. . . .*

The only ones we can trust are each other, insisted Silverthief. *That's how it's always been.* Then Silverthief added, *But that gives me an idea.*

Cara listened. She wasn't sure she liked it, but Silverthief was right—it might work.

After lunch, she found Ellis alone. He was working on his maps, and when Cara entered, he glanced up and smiled.

"Hello! Look!"

He showed her his latest drafts, and Cara nodded, impressed. They were very detailed, showing every part of the hall, with areas marked off "For exploring." She saw the ruins to the north.

"I'd love to investigate that area some more," said Ellis. "Maybe when it's safe?"

"Maybe," said Cara. She looked at his piles of rough copies and pulled out another. "What's this?"

Ellis grinned. "That's the west end of the city!" he said. "It's one of the first maps I ever made. I spent two days exploring every street in the whole of the west quarter. I had to ask my big brother to come with me. It cost me four weeks' worth of pocket money. But isn't it good? There, that's Needle Street. Did you know there used to be a river under there?"

He chatted and pointed, moving over to the hut window to get more light, and Cara asked him questions. But as she talked, she casually reached back, pulled one particular map from the pile, and slipped it down between two desks.

She felt bad—she really did like Ellis—but Silverthief was right. The only people they could trust were each other, and she had to know what was going on.

After dinner, she snuck into the hut, retrieved the map, and headed back toward the ruins. It would be better to wait until darkness, but it wouldn't take Ellis long to notice one of his maps was missing. She checked the map as she walked, trying to memorize it.

The route in had been blocked now. But there was another way, wasn't there? She'd seen another door, on the other side of the chamber. And Ellis had said that he'd found other entrances into the tunnels.

She searched the map and its tiny, detailed comments, and found it. Another way in—an entrance that perhaps even Creedy didn't know about. But Cara would find it, and if it wasn't magically locked . . .

She would learn the truth.

10
THE
PRISONER

The second entrance was where Ellis's map said it would be, near a cluster of stones right against the Guild Hall walls. Cara felt guilty again about stealing his map, but pushed the thought away. This was important. Creedy was lying. Perhaps Berin too. What were they up to, really? What were they planning?

At the entrance she reached in her pack for

a dark lantern, a small lamp with a sliding cover. She lit the lantern, opened the cover enough to let out just a tiny glimmer of light, and slowly walked down the ancient steps. This entrance was like the other, but the roof here had caved in. There was a narrow gap, too small for an adult to fit through. Cara squeezed her way in and entered the tunnels.

She summoned Silverthief, and the dragon whispered into existence.

"Ready?" she asked.

Silverthief sniffed and nodded. "This way," she growled.

Cara felt a thrill run up her spine. It was the same feeling she got every time she started a new mission. The feeling that made it seem like the world was against her. It was just her and Silverthief, the one friend she trusted more than anyone else. It was this thrill that led her to climb sheer walls, to rob the king . . . and to make things deliberately hard for herself.

"Let's go," she whispered, and they ventured into the dark.

The tunnel twisted and branched. Silverthief led her without hesitating. Cara checked the dusty floor but saw no footprints. No one had come this way for decades, perhaps centuries. Her lamp sent a tiny point of light out into the darkness. She picked out more pictures on the walls, carvings, and spots of ancient red paint. A crown, a sword, a city on fire . . .

"Here," whispered Silverthief. Cara saw that they were at a stone doorway like the other one. Another angry stone eye glared at her from above. Her heart sank, but Silverthief seemed excited.

"No magic," Silverthief muttered. "It's not protected. I can sense . . . Ah." She lifted one claw and pushed at an exact point on the door. The door swung inward a few inches and stuck. Cara and the dragon heaved it open and squeezed through.

White sand hissed under Cara's feet, and the air glowed faintly red. She closed her lantern and crept down the tunnel. There was no sound. She moved closer.

The tunnel opened into the chamber. On the far side was the doorway where Creedy had entered. Red jewels glowed above them. Ahead of them was the sarcophagus, the stone coffin with the statue of the woman standing on top. On the other side of the chamber, there were glowing pale-yellow lines that crossed over one another, forming an enormous cage.

Inside the cage was a dragon.

He seemed to be asleep, his snout resting on his two front legs and his long tail curled around himself. He was large, as big as Rockhammer,

and his scales were a soft patchy green. His tail and snout were tinged with gray, and the dragon's skin seemed stretched. He looked very old.

Cara stared and listened to his gentle snoring. A *dragon*. Creedy was keeping a *dragon* prisoner!

"I was right!" hissed Silverthief. "They're up to no good!"

Cara nodded. She walked over to the statue on top of the sarcophagus. It was ancient and coated in a thick layer of dust. It was a woman with long robes and a circlet over her head, almost like a crown. She was holding a stone sword in one hand. Around her neck was an emerald set into an eight-sided stone brooch.

Was this the jewel Creedy had wanted? But then why hadn't he just taken it? Cara turned back to the dragon and stopped.

His eyes were open. He was watching her.

11
JADEHEART

The dragon didn't move at first. Slowly, he examined Cara from top to bottom. Then he lifted his head, stood, and *stretched,* arching his back like a cat. Cara saw that around his neck hung a silver necklace, much larger than the statue's, with a huge emerald. He extended his front claws until they almost touched the yellow bars of his cage.

"You're new," he said in a thick, low growl. "Are you with *him*?"

Cara stared. "Um . . . who?"

The dragon sneered. "*Him. Creedy.* Are you working with him?"

"No." Cara shook her head. "He doesn't know I'm here. Did he capture you? Did he do this?" She waved at the lines that made the cage around him. The dragon nodded.

He stared at Cara. "Why are you here, then?"

"I followed him," said Cara. "Before. What's he doing? Why has he trapped you here?"

She had a sudden thought. Dragons needed humans to summon them and to keep the connection that allowed them to stay in this world. But dragons could leave at any time. Why was this dragon staying in his cage? Why not return to his own world?

"Where's your human?" she asked.

The dragon looked at her, and his face was so sad that Cara felt terrible. She looked at the statue again. "Oh," she said softly. "Is that . . . her?"

The dragon nodded. "Tanora. She was my human, long ago. Long . . . long ago." He nodded again. "I am Jadeheart."

"Cara," said Cara. "And Silverthief."

The dragons nodded to each other.

"I don't understand," said Silverthief. "How can you still be here, in this world?"

Jadeheart shrugged. "I am loyal." He tried

to look toward the statue. Cara realized that from within his cage, he couldn't quite see it.

"What does Creedy want?" Silverthief asked.

Jadeheart tapped the jewel. "This." He gave a sad smile. "A small thing. But it is everything I have, and everything I am."

He sighed. "It was long ago now," he said. "But once, Tanora and I were never apart. She was my human, and I was her dragon."

Cara smiled. "Like me and Silverthief." Silverthief purred.

"Perhaps," said Jadeheart. "She was a

mighty warrior and a magician. I was a king among dragons." His eyes looked misty. "I loved to fly, to carry Tanora into battle. There were so many battles! It was a fearsome time. The time of the Dragon Storm, when humans and dragons fought to save the land—and none fought harder than Tanora and Jadeheart!

"We were always together. We swore never to be apart. Tanora created her greatest magic—she took the bond between us and sealed it, forever, into this jewel. No matter what happened, I would stay in this world with Tanora, forever!

"But"—he scowled—"we were betrayed. Tanora was wounded. She did not recover."

He swung his head in a sad arc. "They buried her here, in this crypt . . . and I stayed with her."

Cara looked around the chamber. "All this time?" she breathed.

"Until *that human* found me." The dragon's lip curled. "Oh, he was so *friendly*—'Oh, great dragon, how *amazing* you are!' But he saw my jewel . . . and he *wanted* it."

Jadeheart waved a paw. " 'Only a look,' he said, but I saw his face. He meant to keep it. He wanted it for himself."

"So he made you a prisoner?" said Silverthief.

"He said he would let me go if I gave up the jewel. But if I do, I will fall from this world and lose Tanora. And if I do not . . ." The dragon reached a claw out toward the crackling yellow lines, and sparks flew up. "I will be trapped forever."

Silverthief hissed like an angry cat, and her skin almost glowed in fury. "How could he do this? It's *awful*!"

"We should tell Berin," said Cara.

"Unless Berin already knows. Unless they're working together!"

Cara chewed her lip. "Yes. . . ."

"Please help me," said Jadeheart. "I just want to see my human's face again."

Cara studied the shimmering cage. "How can we help?"

Silverthief sniffed. "This is powerful magic," she said. "It must be using an anchor. Something . . . *hidden*." She looked around. "Something to hold it in place somewhere . . ."

Cara stared down at the scuffed earth around the cage, and dug through the sand until she felt something slender and strong. It was silver, woven into a thin rope.

"This is it!" she exclaimed. Then she stopped. "Do you hear that?"

Silverthief's ears pricked, and Cara listened. The sound was very faint. It was footsteps, hurrying toward them. It was hard to tell from which direction.

"Creedy!" hissed Silverthief. "He's on his way!"

"Quickly!" said Jadeheart. "Please!"

Cara nodded, lifted the rope, and pulled it apart. There was a noise like a crack, and the yellow lines flared and seemed to widen. They turned as pale as ghosts and passed right through Cara and Silverthief. The girl and dragon flinched, but all they felt was a strange tingle.

Jadeheart stretched again. "Ah . . . Oh, *thank you*." He bounded to the coffin and gazed at the statue. "Oh, Tanora . . ."

"We can go back up the other tunnel," said Cara. "Quick, before he gets here!"

Jadeheart stayed leaning over the sarcophagus, crooning a sad song.

"Jadeheart!" called Cara. "He's coming!"

Jadeheart growled. "Let him come," he hissed. "This time I'll be ready."

Cara and Silverthief swapped worried looks.

"I don't know if that's a good idea," said Silverthief. "Why don't we just slip away?"

The green dragon bowed his head. "Hmm," he said thoughtfully. "Hmm."

Then he made a sound almost like a chuckle.

"I know what you're trying to do," he said. "Do you think I'm a fool?"

Cara blinked. "Um . . . what?"

"I know what you really want," hissed Jadeheart. "Oh, yes. I know what you want, Silver*thief*." The old dragon reared up and glared at them. "You want the jewel for yourselves, don't you? You want to take me away from my human!"

Cara gaped. "No!" she cried. "Really, Jadeheart. You can trust us."

She reached out and patted the dragon's shoulder, and he sighed. Then he swung one paw *fast*, caught Cara, and flung her hard toward the wall!

12

FRIENDS

Cara twisted as she hurtled through the air. She managed to get her feet up to cushion the blow, but she was still winded. Behind her, Silverthief rushed at Jadeheart. The older dragon batted her away like a toy. He stood at his full height, ferocious, with power radiating off him. He seemed to be growing.

"Thieves!" he screamed. "Thieves, come to take my jewel! Come to take my *human*!"

"We're not," croaked Cara, trying to get her breath back. "Jadeheart, you can trust us—"

"I can't trust *any* of you!" he roared. "I can't trust anyone but Tanora! I trusted her and she trusted me! We don't need anyone else!"

Now there were waves of fire flowing from the dragon and flattening Cara against the wall. The walls themselves glowed green, mixing horribly with the red light. Across the chamber, Silverthief picked herself up and shook her head.

"Silver!" shouted Cara. "We have to get out of here!"

Jadeheart's eyes shone with rage. "Oh, no you don't!" he roared. "Thieves must be *punished*!"

He took a deep breath and ROARED. The flames grew even higher.

"You want to split us apart!" he screamed. "You're like all the others!"

"We're not!" yelled Cara. "I promise!"

"Liars!"

He swung his tail around in a high arc, and Cara dodged it.

"Villains!"

"CARA!" roared a voice. She spun around to see Ellis and Pathseeker come crashing into the chamber.

"Ellis?"

"Cara, what's going on?" Ellis bellowed. Behind him were Mira and Flameteller and Tom and Ironskin!

"More of you?" spat Jadeheart. "Come to attack me! Come to steal my jewel!"

"Watch out!" shouted Cara as the huge green dragon drew a breath and ROARED again. Green flames shot out and over Ellis, and Cara covered her mouth in horror.

"Ellis!"

But to her astonishment, the flames didn't touch him. And now she saw Ironskin's face fixed in concentration, and she remembered—this was Ironskin's special power, to create a shield! The green flames blistered against it but couldn't get through.

Cara turned back to Jadeheart and noticed the jewel again. It was pulsing horribly. Jadeheart grew larger with every pulse, as if feeding off it—but somehow it seemed to be feeding off him too.

"Jadeheart!" she shouted. "I think the jewel is doing something to you!"

"Lies."

"We're dragonseers, Jadeheart! We're like Tanora! Trust us!"

Jadeheart shifted between Cara and the other children, as if deciding whom to attack first. He brought his tail around in a mighty sweep, and it crashed into the others, driving them away from the doorway. He bellowed again.

"Cara!" hissed Silverthief. "We can go!"

Cara gaped. "What?"

"Look! We can make it out!" Cara turned and saw what she meant. Jadeheart was distracted by the other children, who were now halfway around the chamber, away from the doorway. There was a gap!

"But what about the others?"

"That great lout Ironskin has her magic

shield protecting them. They'll be fine," said Silverthief. "Come on!"

She shoved Cara toward the doorway, and they dived out. Cara turned back for a moment and watched Jadeheart's flames attacking Ironskin's shield. It was still holding. The other dragons, Pathseeker and Flameteller, seemed to be trying to talk to Jadeheart, without much success.

"Come *on!*" hissed Silverthief.

Cara stumbled down the hallway. "Why was Ellis there?" she panted. "And Tom and Mira?"

Silverthief snorted. "Who cares? All that matters is you and me!"

The exit was ahead, its dim light growing as they got closer. This close to the edge of the hall, the globes were sparse and dim. Hardly anyone came out this far. No wonder Ellis was the only other one to discover the second entrance.

Cara stopped running. "*That's* why they're here," she muttered. "Ellis must have noticed we took the map."

Silverthief said, "So he wanted it back, right? Didn't want you exploring! Typical!"

"No," said Cara. "I mean, I think he came for me. . . . Silver, I think they came to rescue us!"

"What?" hissed the dragon. "Why would they do *that*? Come on!"

But Cara stood still. "They came to get us,"

she said stubbornly. "They thought we might get into trouble, and they came to rescue us. They were . . . Ellis is . . ." She hesitated. "Silver, I think Ellis is my friend."

"What?!" Now the dragon looked furious. "Cara, *I'm* your friend!"

"Yes, of course! But maybe Ellis is too?"

Silverthief shook her head. "No, no. It's you and me, Cara. It always has been! The only people we can trust are each other!"

Cara looked at her. "Yes," she said. And then: "No. That's what Jadeheart said. That's what he said about his human, but he's *wrong*. Don't you understand?"

Silverthief stared at her with a baffled expression. "No. I can't. . . ."

"Yes," said Cara firmly. "Yes, Silver. Look. You trust me, yes?"

"Yes, always!"

"Then trust me now. Ellis is . . . *our friend.* Mira is our friend. Tom is our friend. They invited us to go exploring. Ellis showed me the maps. They came to *rescue* us. They're our *friends*!"

She gasped. "And we've left them in danger!"

She spun and ran back down the passage, toward the chamber and the shouting.

"Wait!" cried Silverthief, but Cara ignored her. "Cara, wait!"

13
POWERS

Cara burst back into the chamber and threw her hands up against her face. The flames were worse than ever! In the center, Jadeheart was howling and shrieking and throwing balls of green fire at the other children and dragons. He'd blocked off their escape, and now they were huddled under Ironskin's magical shield. Flameteller and Pathseeker kept darting out, trying to talk to Jadeheart or distract him, but with no luck.

"Thieves!" howled Jadeheart. "Traitors!"

He seemed unaware of Cara. She tried to figure out what to do. Distract him? But then what? He was growing even larger, and at his chest the jewel glowed a sick bright green, thrumming with power.

The jewel . . .

She had to get the jewel. She looked at Jadeheart's hide, covered in rough scales. Could she climb up the tail? It was a wild idea, but she didn't know what else to do. She took a deep breath and got ready to run.

Something crashed down on her back, and she collapsed to the floor. She spun and stared up into the eyes of Silverthief. The dragon's face was furious and confused.

"What are you *doing*?" Silverthief hissed.

"Trying to get the jewel! It's where his power comes from!"

"It's too risky! You could get hurt!" Silverthief looked as if she was about to cry. "Why are you doing this, Cara? Why are you doing this to me? To us?"

Ironskin's shield was weakening. There was so little time! But Cara tried to stay calm. She looked into Silverthief's eyes and spoke as gently as she could.

"Silver, they're our *friends*. We're not used to that, but they are. I trust you. You trust me. *We can trust them*. And they're in trouble. We have to help." She smiled. "It's what friends do."

Silverthief shook her head. For a moment she seemed about to howl. But then she sighed.

"But . . . then . . . are *we* still friends?"

Cara hugged the dragon tight around her neck. "Silver, you're the best friend I could ever have!"

Silverthief sighed again. "Well. Well, good." She almost looked embarrassed. Then her eyes widened. "Wait—I can feel what to do!"

She stood up and closed her eyes. She began to sway slightly.

"Silver?"

"Shh!"

Silverthief's skin was a mix of red and green,

matching the colors around her. But now she seemed fainter. Suddenly Cara realized she wasn't seeing Silverthief at all—she was seeing *through* her! The dragon was disappearing, becoming invisible, until only the faint silver glow of her edges remained.

Cara reached out to touch Silverthief and gasped. Her own hand was the same! She could see through it to the ground below. It was faintly white, like a ghost, and getting paler and paler. . . .

"Is this your power?" she breathed.

"I think so. I think I

can do it for me and for you too." The faint outline of her face grinned. "Come on—let's be heroes!"

Cara leaped onto Silverthief's back. It was a weird sensation, as if she was sitting on nothing. And then it got much worse as Silverthief took a few steps and launched herself into the air. Cara clung to an invisible neck and tried not to look down. Heights didn't bother her, but this was something else!

"I'll get as close as I'm able to," muttered Silverthief. She flew toward Jadeheart, avoiding his huge green claws. She wasn't a very good flier. Cara was tossed from side to side. She held on desperately.

"Ready?" hissed Silverthief. "You'll have to jump!"

Cara gulped, lifted her feet, and crouched on Silverthief's back. One . . . two . . .

Three!

She leaped forward and caught hold of the huge silver necklace with one hand. Now she was dangling from the dragon's neck.

Jadeheart peered down. "Who's that?"

Cara was still invisible, but Jadeheart could feel her. One claw swung around, and Cara dodged to the side, still holding the chain. She scrambled for the jewel.

There it was—an eight-sided silver brooch with a brilliant green stone glowing inside.

Cara wasn't sure what to do next. The chain was as thick as her wrist, heavy and solid. The brooch looked secure.

"Watch out!" shouted Silverthief, and Cara swung again as another claw batted at her.

"Who's there?!" roared Jadeheart again. "Thief! I can *feel* you!"

There was only one thing to do.

"I'm sorry," whispered Cara. She whipped her knife out from her boot, flipped it around, and smashed its base against the jewel.

She wasn't sure what she expected. She hoped she would knock the jewel out of its setting. But to her surprise, the emerald shattered at once. It had seemed strong, but inside it was rotten. The green flames around them collapsed, and Jadeheart gasped.

"Nooooo!"

He staggered and seemed to shrink. Cara dangled on the chain by one hand, then let go, curled, and landed in a crouch.

"Cara!" shouted Silverthief.

Cara held up a hand. "I'm okay," she gasped before turning to Jadeheart.

Already the dragon was back to the size he'd been when Cara had first found him. He was scrabbling around at the floor of the chamber, trying to scrape together the tiny pieces of shattered jewel and making a horrible, sad wail.

Cara walked toward him.

"Stay back!" warned Silverthief, but she kept going.

Now Jadeheart was only as big as Ironskin.

"Tanora," he mumbled. "Tanora!" He stumbled over to the tomb and gazed down.

"I'm sorry," whispered Cara. Awkwardly she reached up and patted the creature's flanks.

The dragon sobbed. "It wasn't the same, you know. After she was gone. The jewel reminded me of her. But it wasn't the same. It . . ." He looked surprised. "Oh, I attacked you all! Oh, dear!"

"It was the jewel," said Cara. "It wasn't you."

"Tanora wouldn't have wanted that!" he

cried. Now he was only a little taller than Cara.

"It's okay," said Cara. "She'll understand."

Jadeheart sniffed. "What will happen now?"

The other dragons limped forward.

"You'll return to our world," said Flameteller.

Jadeheart frowned. "It's been so long . . . ," he whispered.

Pathseeker smiled. "It's easy," she said. "We'll come with you and show you the way."

Ironskin said, "And then you can dream."

Jadeheart looked up hopefully. "Will I . . . remember her?"

"Always," said Silverthief. "She was your

141

best friend, and you were hers. You'll remember her forever."

Jadeheart sighed. He was fading now. "I'd like that," he whispered. "I'd like . . ."

And then he was gone, and the other dragons too, and the chamber was silent.

14
FAMILY

The children squeezed back through the entrance and returned to the surface.

"Uh-oh," said Ellis.

Cara looked up and groaned. Creedy was stalking toward them. He held his staff up high, the yellow light flaring off it. His face was furious. Behind him was Berin.

Creedy glared at them. "And just what do you think you're doing here?" he demanded.

The children looked at each other. Cara realized they were a mess—their hair was scorched, their clothes torn, their hands scratched and black with soot.

"Exploring?" said Ellis tentatively.

Creedy bristled. "Didn't I give strict instructions—"

"It's not their fault," said Cara. "It's mine. I went . . . exploring, and got into trouble."

Now Berin was with them. She examined them carefully. "Is everyone all right?"

"Oh, yes," said Cara, and smiled. "My friends rescued me."

There was a lot of shouting. A *lot*. First, Creedy shouted at them all for a while. Then he went to explore the chamber, and Berin spoke to them in a serious, disappointed voice, until Cara thought she would prefer to be shouted at. And then Creedy came back from the chamber and *did* shout at them again, for even longer this time.

Finally they were sent off to Hilda, the nurse and cook. She clucked over their scratches, gave them buckets of hot water to wash with, and served them slices of bread straight from the oven with butter and new jam. Then she sent them off to bed.

The next day, Cara was summoned to Berin's office. When she got there, Berin was waiting, and Malik too. He nodded to her, but his face looked unusually serious.

Berin sat. Cara stood.

"Vice Chancellor Creedy has given me his report," said Berin. "It appears he found the chamber some weeks ago, and Jadeheart too."

"He kept him prisoner," said Cara.

Berin pursed her lips. "The vice chancellor says that Jadeheart became violent and had to be restrained. He was trying to get Jadeheart to hand over the jewel voluntarily. He thought this might be better."

Cara said nothing. Berin sighed. "Tanora and Jadeheart were heroes once, you know," she said softly. "Legends, even. They fought in the Dragon Storm war and saved many lives. They were never apart. Their link was so strong, Jadeheart lived almost entirely in this world.

"The jewel was well meant, but it changed them both. Toward the end, Tanora was . . . different. And poor Jadeheart too."

Cara said, "When I smashed the jewel, he seemed to change."

"Hmm. Is there anything else I should know?"

Cara hesitated.

Should we tell them? said Silverthief's voice in her mind. *We might get into trouble. . . .*

Cara took a deep breath. "Well . . . when I met Malik . . . at the palace—"

Dragon Storm

"While you were *robbing* the palace," said Berin in a level voice.

Cara coughed. "Um . . . yeah. The thing is, there was this rumor going around downtown, about the king. About this special jewel he had, worth more than the entire kingdom. I mean, that's what folk said."

Berin gazed at Cara.

"So, um, that's what I was there for," said Cara. "And I found it. I didn't take it! But . . . it was like the jewel Jadeheart had. Only it wasn't green. It was a diamond with eight sides. And there was a . . ." She hesitated. "An *eye* in it. Like, a *real eye*. It moved."

Berin and Malik stared at her.

"So King Godfic has a Dragon's Eye,"

148

said Malik. He whistled. "Now, *that's* interesting."

Berin nodded. "Thank you, Cara. Anything else?"

Cara shook her head.

"Right." Berin studied her. "Well, Malik is here to take you back to the city. So, thank you for spending time with us, and good luck with your life."

Cara started. "What?"

Berin looked surprised. "Well, that's what you want, isn't it? To leave?"

She sighed. "Cara, you broke the rules, more than once. You put the others in danger. You *stole* from Ellis. And . . . you just don't seem to be happy here.

"This isn't a prison, you know. You can leave. Malik will help. We can give you a little money or find you a foster home—a good home, with good people. It's up to you. You can leave whenever you want."

She studied Cara. "*Is* that what you want?"

We could leave, said Silverthief. *We could leave, Cara!*

Cara said nothing.

That would be best, wouldn't it? Silverthief's voice wasn't quite so certain as usual. *I suppose Pathseeker is all right. And Ironskin's Protection magic was good. But we don't need them. Flameteller's quite nice when you get to know him. But, I mean . . .* She trailed off.

Cara said slowly, "Would it be all right if I . . . if I stayed here? Maybe a little longer?"

Berin raised an eyebrow. "Oh?"

"Well . . . ," said Cara awkwardly. "I mean, my friends are here."

Berin looked back down at her paperwork. "Of course," she said.

Cara nodded. That seemed to be it. She turned to leave.

"Oh, Cara?" said Berin.

Cara turned back.

Berin smiled. "Welcome to the family."

THE DRAGON STORM IS COMING.

Soar into adventure with dragonseer

Ellis and his dragon, Pathseeker!

The Master Gardener continued. "If any children would like to take part, and be the first to attempt to solve the Three Mazes, then come forward now and take your flag!"

Ellis, Cara, and Connor came forward, as well as a few local children. They approached a table in front of the stage. The table was covered in flags of different colors, each one on a long stick. A smiling woman in green took each child's name and gave them a flag.

"Now," she said, "the maze walls are quite

tall, but if you get lost, just wave this as high as you can, and we'll come and find you, all right?"

Ellis took his flag, the same shade of green as Pathseeker. "I won't need it," he said.

The woman laughed. "I wouldn't be too sure," she said. "We've had some fun designing this year's mazes!"

When they had their flags, the children lined up in front of the first challenge: the Green Maze.

The Green Maze was made of tall box hedges cut into beautiful neat walls. It had three entrances, and the contestants lined up around them. There were about thirty children, grinning and laughing, some fooling around. Ellis checked his backpack again, pulled out his new notebook and a pencil stub, then held his breath.

"The Green Maze!" called the speaker. "Brave adventurers, enter if you dare! Find your way to the very center, collect the ribbon of your color, and escape the maze. First contestant out with their ribbon is the winner! Are you ready?"

Ellis glanced at Cara and Connor, and they grinned back.

"Steady?"

Ellis leaned forward over the starting line.

"Go!"